Especially for baby Arthur, with love
~ M C B

For my cousin Jessica Smith
~ T M

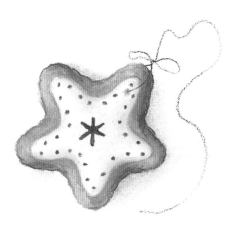

LITTLE TIGER PRESS LTD,
an imprint of the Little Tiger Group
1 The Coda Centre,
189 Munster Road, London SW6 6AW
www.littletiger.co.uk
First published in Great Britain 2017
Text copyright © M Christina Butler 2017
Illustrations copyright © Tina Macnaughton 2017

M Christina Butler and Tina Macnaughton have asserted
their rights to be identified as the author and illustrator of this
work under the Copyright, Designs and Patents Act, 1988

A CIP catalogue record for this book is available from the British Library
All rights reserved • ISBN 978-1-84869-669-3
Printed in China • LTP/1800/1819/0217
10 9 8 7 6 5 4 3 2 1

One Cosy Christmas

M Christina Butler • Tina Macnaughton

LiTTLE TiGER

LONDON

It was a crisp winter's day and Little Hedgehog and his friends were looking for a Christmas tree.

"This one! This one!" squeaked the baby mice.

"Perfect!" beamed Little Hedgehog. "I'm so pleased you could all stay for Christmas. It's going to be wonderful!"

"Oh, Christmas tree,
Oh, Christmas tree,
How evergreen
your branches,"
the mice sang merrily
on the way home.

Everyone helped with the
decorations, and soon the
tree sparkled in the lamplight.
"Well, isn't this lovely?" sighed
Little Hedgehog.
"Hooray for Christmas with friends!"
they all cheered on their way to bed.

But in the morning everyone was in a terrible mood!
"Ouch!" cried Fox. "You trod on my paws!"
"I can't find my socks!" moaned Rabbit.
"Never mind your socks!" grumbled Badger.
"Who was snoring all night long?"

"And who's been eating the decorations?" squeaked a baby mouse. "We hung seven biscuits on the tree yesterday, and now there's only six!"

"Stop!" cried Little Hedgehog.
"We mustn't squabble at
Christmas! Let's do
something fun. Shall
we go skating?"

"Yes, please," agreed the
baby mice and they all
set off to the pond.

Sliding and gliding across the ice, the friends were soon laughing again. They twirled until they were quite tired out. Then, with frosty paws, they skated home.

As he warmed up with cookies and cocoa,
Little Hedgehog smiled to himself.
"I can't wait for Christmas!" he thought.

"I hope you sleep well, Badger," said
Little Hedgehog as they headed to bed.
   "Thank you," yawned Badger. "Let's hope
there won't be any more snoring."

But in the morning the friends were grumpier than ever!

"That snoring was awful!" harrumphed Badger.

"I was awake all night!" Fox snapped.

"Excuse me, Fox," grumbled Mouse.

"You're squashing my Christmas jumper!"

But that wasn't all . . .

"Someone's eaten another biscuit!" called a baby mouse.

"Wait! Something even more terrible's happened!" cried Little Hedgehog. "I can't find my HAT!"

"This will never do!" said Rabbit. "We must find Little Hedgehog's hat!"

But although they searched high and low all morning . . .

they couldn't find it anywhere!

Little Hedgehog watched sadly as the mice played in the snow. It was too cold to go outside without his hat.

"I can't even go in my own kitchen," he sniffed, "because Fox is baking a surprise. Perhaps Christmas won't be perfect after all!"

At suppertime, as he tucked into Fox's delicious cake, Little Hedgehog began to feel a little better. The tree twinkled in the firelight and Badger told thrilling tales of the wild wood.

"It's nearly Christmas!" giggled the baby mice excitedly, clapping their paws.
But poor Little Hedgehog was still thinking about his hat. "It's such a mystery!" he mumbled.

That night Little Hedgehog hardly slept a wink.
The house echoed with giggles, squeaks, and
a strange click-clicking sound.

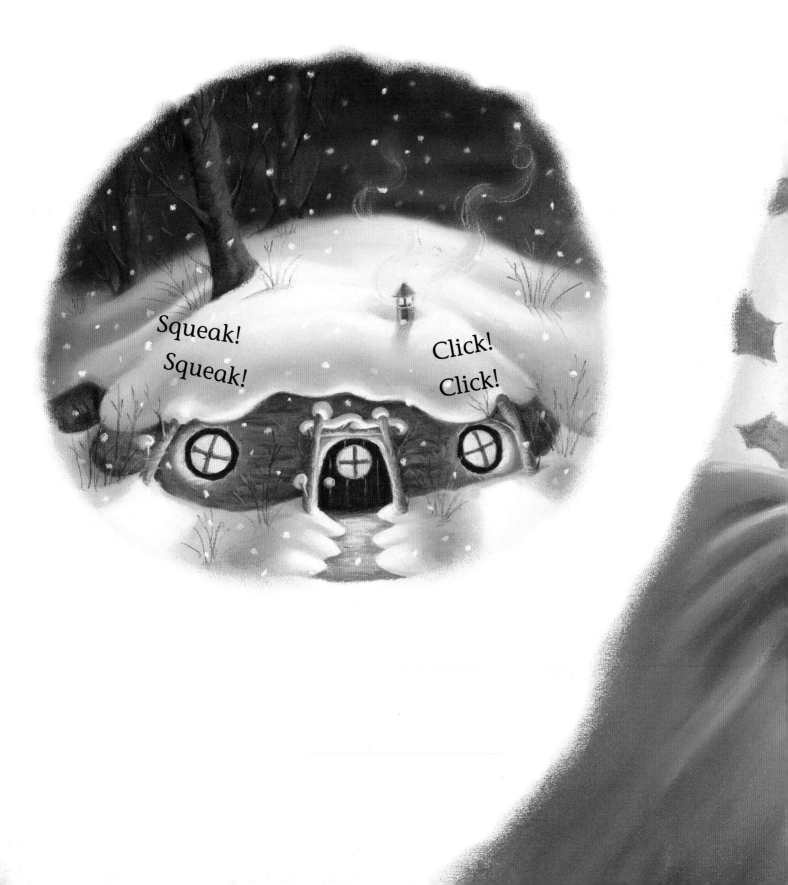

But when the first rays of the morning
sun peeped through his curtains,
Little Hedgehog leapt out of bed.
  "It's Christmas morning!" he cried happily,
completely forgetting how sleepy he was.

"Happy Christmas, everyone!" sang Little Hedgehog as the friends gathered to open their presents.

"We stayed up to paint you this picture!" squeaked the baby mice.

"And this is from me!" smiled Badger.

"What a lovely new hat, Badger!" cried Little Hedgehog. "That clicking noise last night was your knitting needles!"

Everyone was merrily
unwrapping their gifts
when all of a sudden
Mouse cried, "Goodness me!
The Christmas tree is
snoring!"

"Whatever could it be?" cried Little Hedgehog.
And when he looked he had such a surprise!
"Well I never!" he murmured. "I've found my
hat . . . and there's someone asleep inside it!"

The friends looked down at a little snoozing squirrel.
"He must have been hibernating in the tree when
we brought it home!" whispered Badger.
"That explains the snoring!" exclaimed Fox.
"And the missing biscuits!"

"Well, I'm glad my old hat found a good home," smiled Little Hedgehog. "How wonderful to share Christmas with my dearest friends . . . and a brand new friend too!"